MW00954781

Kenny dog and Dio frog play outside

by LaToya Linen

To my boys
Nazavier, Kendrick, and D'Angelo

K enny Dog and Di
breakfast t

Frog eat a yummy
start the day

All finished they go
outside to play

They Say hi to the b
Dio frog jumps and h

Kenny Dog runs super fast

Kenn
lo

Dog and Dio Frog
ve being outside

Slide down
the slide swing
on the swings

Play with s
Side
kites,

o many magical things.
walk chalk, cars,
bubbles and balls.

Pick flowers,
launch
jump rope, p
on tramp-
in b

Build Towers out of blocks,
rockets, Hop scotch,
aint rocks, Jump jump high
line, stomp stomp jump
ig muddy puddles.

Leap in leaves
and play in snow

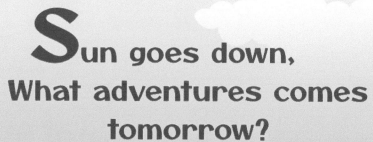

Sun goes down,
What adventures comes
tomorrow?

Sidewalk C

1 PART WATER, 1 PART CORNS

MIX TOGETHER THE WATER AND CORNSTARCH, SPLIT UP THE

Chalk paint

TARCH, AND FOOD COLORING

MIXTURE INTO CUPS, AND ADD COLOR

CLOUD

- 8 cups all-purpose flour
- 1 cup baby oil.
  Put all ingredients into a
  flour, mix until well inco
  for outside play

DOUGH

not gluten free

a bowl. Combine the baby oil and
rporated. Put it in a large container

Playdough recipe

3 cups all-purpose white flour
2 tablespoons cream of tartar
1 cup + 2 tablespoons table salt
3–4 tablespoons cooking oil
3 cups hot water
Optional: Food coloring

Cook over medium heat, stirring constantly, until forms a soft ball.
Remove from heat and roll in a ball. Put in Ziploc bag
Or cover with plastic wrap and let cool
split into portions and color with food coloring

Enjoy!!

SNOW PAINT RECIPE

INGREDIENTS

water, food coloring, and bottles

First fill your spray bottles or squeeze bottles with water. add 5-7 drops of concentrated food coloring to each bottle. Go have fun painting snow!

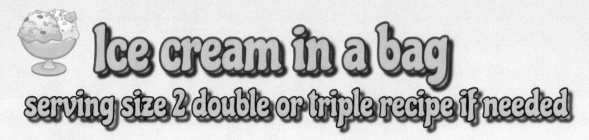

Ice cream in a bag
serving size 2 double or triple recipe if needed

1 cup half and half
1.5 tsp vanilla extract
1 tbsp sugar
ice
1/4 cup salt
Ziploc bags 1 large 1 small
strawberry or chocolate syrup(optional)

Pour 1 cup of half and half, Add 1.5 teaspoons of vanilla extract, sugar.
in small ziplock add chocolate or strawberry syrup to flavor (Optional)
get any excess air out of bag and seal
In large ziplock bag, combine ice and salt.
10 to 15 minutes, or until ice cream has hardened.
scoop out of and enjoy

outdoor scavenger hunt ✨

a circle

something green

something red

a stick

a leaf

something that makes you happy 😊

something yellow 🤍

a bird 🐦

something brown

a cloud ☁️

a tree 🌲

a flower 🌼

water 💧

a bug 🐛

Gummy worm popcicles

Gummy sour worms or regular gummy worms
your favorite juice
popsicles molds or paper/plastic cups with popsicle sticks

Put some gummy worms in popsicle molds

Fill popsicle molds with juice, freeze until frozen solid

Mini Muffin Pancake Bites

ingredients

Pancake batter (your favorite)
Toppings (blueberries, bananas, chocolate chips
strawberries, sprinkles, cinnamon/sugar)
Non-stick cooking spray
Mini muffin pan

Preheat oven 350 degrees. Spray muffin pan with nonstick cooking spray then set aside.
make pancake batter(follow instructions on box) fill each muffin tin a little over 1/2 way.
add favorite topping (kid love adding the toppings) Bake about 15-20 minutes.

Fun things to do outside

Fly a kite ✦ build a bird feeder ✦
Go on nature walk ✦ play
hopscotch ✦ play catch ✦ jump
rope ✦ bird watch ✦ pick flowers
✦ paint rocks ✦ blow
bubbles ✦ make sidewalk art ✦ bike
ride ✦ visit zoo ✦ jump in pile of
leaves ✦ stargazing ✦ geocaching
✦ visit a farm ✦ feed ducks ✦
berry or apple picking ✦
sledding ✦ go swimming ✦ paint
snow ✦ make leave art ✦ have a
picnic ✦ scavenger hunt ✦ make
mud pies ✦ play in the rain ✦

NOTE FROM THE AUTHOR

Thank you so much for spending time to read my book.

I would really appreciate it if you could:

Review this. Reviews, even very brief ones, are a huge help to new authors. If you enjoyed this story and don't mind sharing your opinion, please consider leaving a review on Amazon.

Share this. When you share this book on social media, you're letting more people discover this story. And word-of-mouth is the best marketing for a budding author.

Thank you!

LaToya

Kenny dog & Dio frog

Coming Soon!!

ABOUT
AUTHOR

LATOYA LINEN

LaToya Linen is a mom of three boys who always had a passion for creativity. Along with writing children's books she enjoys cooking, photography, painting, cake decorating, and party planning. She was inspired by her sons to create stories about things they enjoy doing together.

CPSIA information can be obtained
at www.ICGtesting.com
Printed in the USA
BVHW022321310821
615694BV00002B/21

9 781087 901237